My Mouth Is A Volcano!

Activity and idea Book

published by

NATIONAL CENTER for YOUTH ISSUES

A Note To Parents and Educators

Unnecessary interrupting is an annoying behavior that is quite common in the classroom. Most students don't intend to be rude when they interrupt. They just believe they have something to say, and their need to get their immediate point across outweighs their will to control their response.

Interrupting is a behavior that children learn at a young age. Early in life, all children believe the entire world revolves around them. This egocentric mindset encourages impulsive thinking and consequently leads to interrupting as a way of meeting the child's immediate needs or wants.

Older children and adults interrupt for various reasons. They may like being the center of attention, they may not have the ability or desire to curb their impulsiveness, they may be convinced that they need to "blurt out" an immediate solution to a problem, or they may have just plain old "bad manners." Whatever the reason, interrupting is detrimental to the development of good interpersonal relationships. When people interrupt, they send the message that the ideas and thoughts of others are less important than theirs.

Parents and teachers attempt to discourage interrupting but often find themselves responding to the interrupting child, which in turn may perpetuate the problem.

This workbook is designed to offer students "hands on" activities that explore interrupting. The activities address the reasons people interrupt, when interrupting is necessary, how unnecessary interrupting makes people feel, how to interrupt politely and how and when to stop yourself from interrupting.

Duplication and Copyright

NATIONAL CENTER for
YOUTH ISSUES

P.O. Box 22185
Chattanooga, TN 37422-2185
423.899.5714 • 866.318.6294
fax: 423.899.4547
www.ncyi.org

ISBN: 978-1-931636-91-9
© 2009 National Center for Youth Issues, Chattanooga, TN
All rights reserved.

Summary: A supplementary teacher's guide for *My Mouth Is A Volcano*. Full of discussion questions and exercises to share with students.

Written by: Julia Cook
Illustrations by: Carrie Hartman
Published by National Center for Youth Issues

Printed at Starkey Printing
Chattanooga, TN, USA
February 2018

THINK ABOUT IT...

Someone Interrupted Me!

1. Write about a time when someone interrupted you.

2. How did that make you feel?

3. What did you think of the person who interrupted?

4. Was the interruption necessary? Why or why not?

5. Could the person who interrupted you have handled the situation differently?
   If so, what could he or she have done?

THINK ABOUT IT...TOO

I Interrupted Someone Else!

1. Write about a time when you interrupted someone.

2. Why did you do it?

3. How did you feel right after you did it?

4. Was the interruption necessary?

5. What could you have done instead of interrupting?

6. If you could do it all over again, would you still have interrupted? Why or why not?

PUZZLE ERUPT

This activity is designed to allow students to feel the frustrations associated with being interrupted. If they can develop an understanding of what it feels like to be interrupted, they may think twice before interrupting others.

Materials Needed
• Several 100-piece jigsaw puzzles (enough for approximately 4 kids to puzzle)
• Floor Space
• Desirable reward for winning team (extra recess time, milkshake pass, candy bars, etc.)

Directions
1. Divide the class into teams of 4 to 5.
2. Give each team a puzzle and explain that they are to work together to complete the puzzle. The first team to complete the puzzle wins the reward. (The puzzle must remain in their boxes until you say GO!)
3. Once the students are engaged in this activity, begin interrupting them! Use several of the following strategies, or think of others that uniquely fit your classroom. The more interruptions, the more effective this activity will be.

Interrupting Strategies
• Pull two involved students from one group and place them in another group. Repeat several times.
• Pull two involved students from a group and talk with them about an irrelevant previous or upcoming assignment.
• Shut off your classroom lights and say, "OOPS! I accidentally hit the switch."
• Call the entire class to attention and discuss with them an irrelevant detail about an upcoming event.
• Pre-arrange several interruptions form the office.
• Start this activity just prior to a scheduled fire drill.
• Start singing.
• Tell students that their time is up before they have had a chance to complete their puzzles and then attempt to move on to another activity.

Classroom Discussion
Ask your students the following questions and discuss the answers as a class. (Questions may vary so that they fit the interruption strategies used.)

1. How did it make you feel when I took you from your group and moved you to another group? How did your group react?
2. How did you feel when I pulled you out of your group and asked you questions?
3. Did my questions have anything to do with the class activity?
4. Could those questions have been asked at a better time?
5. When the fire alarm went off, how did you feel?
6. Was this interruption necessary or important? Why?
7. When I started to sing, how did you react? What did you think about?
8. When I tried to change activities before you were finished, how did you feel? Was my interruption necessary? Could it have been avoided?

After exploring these questions with your students, arrive at the conclusion that there are times when interrupting is necessary (fire drills, etc.). Other times, however, interrupting is irritating and unnecessary. Discuss how stopping to think before you interrupt can help reduce interrupting.

ABILITY BAGS

This activity will give students the opportunity to share their unique abilities and to practice their good listening skills.

Materials Needed
- One small paper sack for each child (lunch bag size)
- Crayons and markers

Directions

1. Have students colorfully decorate their bags with the words "My Ability Bag!"

2. Instruct students to fill their bag with five items from home that represent their abilities. Examples include: a picture of a younger sibling (the ability to be a great big brother), a favorite book (the ability to be a good reader) or a craft (the ability to make things).

3. Send bags home along with the parent letter (next page). Just copy the letter and cut in half giving one letter to each student. Make sure to specify when you need the ability bags filled and returned.

4. When all the students have returned their bags, have them sit in a circle with their bags in the floor in front of them. Placing their bags in their laps may cause too many distractions.

5. Have students take turns removing one item from their bag and explaining it to the class by saying, "I have the ability to _____."

6. Practice good listening skills and praise students for not interrupting. If interrupting does take place, kindly explain to students that since what they are saying is not an emergency, they will have to wait their turn.

7. After everyone has shared their abilities, ask students to recall the abilities of their classmates. Point out similarities of abilities and celebrate uniqueness among your students.

Note

Ability bags are a great way for students and teachers to get to know each other. This activity helps students respect others, develop good listening skills, and break the habit of interrupting.

It may work well for older children to share all five abilities at one time before moving on to the next student. Younger children, however, respond more effectively to sharing one item at a time and rotating through the circle five times.

Allow students who fail to return their ability bags in time to fill another bag with items from your classroom that represent personal strengths and abilities.

Dear Parents,

Today, your child is bringing home his or her ABILITY BAG.

Please help your child fill it with 5 items that symbolize his or her abilities. (For example, a picture of a younger sibling may symbolize the ability to be a GREAT big brother or a craft your child has made could represent the ability to make things). Each child will share his or her abilities with the class.

Please make sure that all items fit in the bag. All items will be placed back in the ability bags as soon as they are shared and will be returned home that day.

This activity will help our class develop better listening skills, help us appreciate and celebrate our unique differences, and give us all a chance to learn more about each other.

We will be sharing our ability bags on: _____.

Please make sure your child brings his or her bag prior to our sharing date. Bags will be collected as they are brought in and saved until our special day.

Dear Parents,

Today, your child is bringing home his or her ABILITY BAG.

Please help your child fill it with 5 items that symbolize his or her abilities. (For example, a picture of a younger sibling may symbolize the ability to be a GREAT big brother or a craft your child has made could represent the ability to make things). Each child will share his or her abilities with the class.

Please make sure that all items fit in the bag. All items will be placed back in the ability bags as soon as they are shared and will be returned home that day.

This activity will help our class develop better listening skills, help us appreciate and celebrate our unique differences, and give us all a chance to learn more about each other.

We will be sharing our ability bags on: _____.

Please make sure your child brings his or her bag prior to our sharing date. Bags will be collected as they are brought in and saved until our special day.

DESIGN A VOLCANO T-SHIRT

Directions:

Use your creativity to design a T-Shirt for Louis to wear that will remind him not to interrupt. You may wish to cut these out and display them on a bulletin board.

Remember what Louis' mom told him to do when he wanted to interrupt:

"When your words are pushed into your teeth by your tongue..."

- Bite down really hard
- Breathe your words out through your nose
- Wait until the other person has finished talking and
- Breathe your words back into your mouth

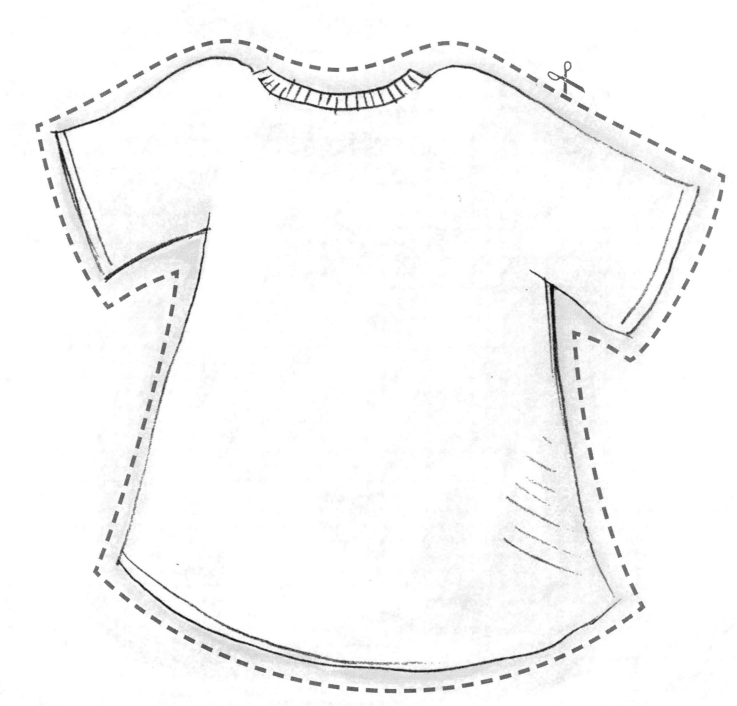

STICK TO IT!

The Purpose of "STICK TO IT!" is to give your students a visual representation of how interrupting affects learning in school and communicating with friends.

Materials Needed:
- light-weight wooden blocks
- Markers
- Glue

Directions:
1. Using markers, label two blocks "**My Brain**."
2. Label the other two blocks "**Your Brain**."
3. Label the bottle of glue "**Important Information**." Explain to your students that the glue represents important information that is traveling from your brain to their brain in an educational environment or important information between friends in a social environment.
4. Glue both sides of the blocks together. Leave one set alone and let it dry. This set represents situations in which you are teaching or friends are talking without being interrupted.
5. Take the other set of blocks and pull them apart several times throughout the drying process. Explain to your students that each time you pull the blocks apart, it represents an interruption. The first set of blocks will have a strong bond, which represents successful listening and learning. The second set of blocks will not be bonded and will have a weak bond with glue stuck on each block. This represents unsuccessful listening and learning and incomplete communication.

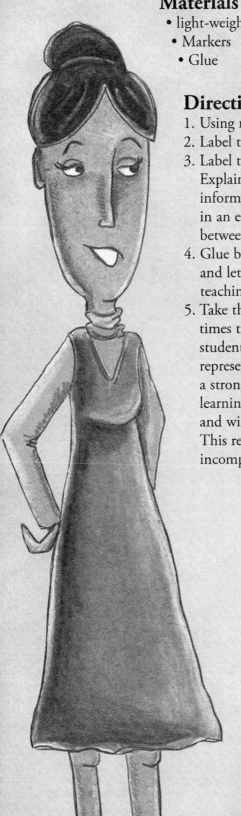

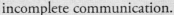

BUTTON UP!

Visual reminders are KEY when teaching children not to interrupt. If there are times when you want to directly teach without being interrupted with questions or comments, you may want to use Button Up!

Materials Needed for Each Child:
• One large button or drawing of a button
• (2) 3x5 blank index cards for each child
• Glue
• Black permanent marker
• Crayons (red and green)

Directions:
1. Have students color one index card green and the other red.
2. Glue the index cards together, color sides out.
3. On the green side, have students write "Speak With Good Purpose" using the black permanent marker.
4. Glue the button to the red side. (Make sure they glue the button slightly to the left side to make room for the next step.)
5. Using the black permanent marker, have students draw an arrow pointing up just to the right side of the button.

Secure one side of the card with tape to the corner of the students' desks so that they can flip it back and forth as needed. When you want to teach without interrupting students place the red Button Up side of the card, face up on their desk. When you tell them to flip the card over to the green side they may ask questions and make comments.

a NOBLE INTERRUPTION

Interrupting is necessary at times, and there is a correct and polite way to do it! In each of the spaces in the shield below, draw a picture illustrating the step leading to a correct and polite way to interrupt.

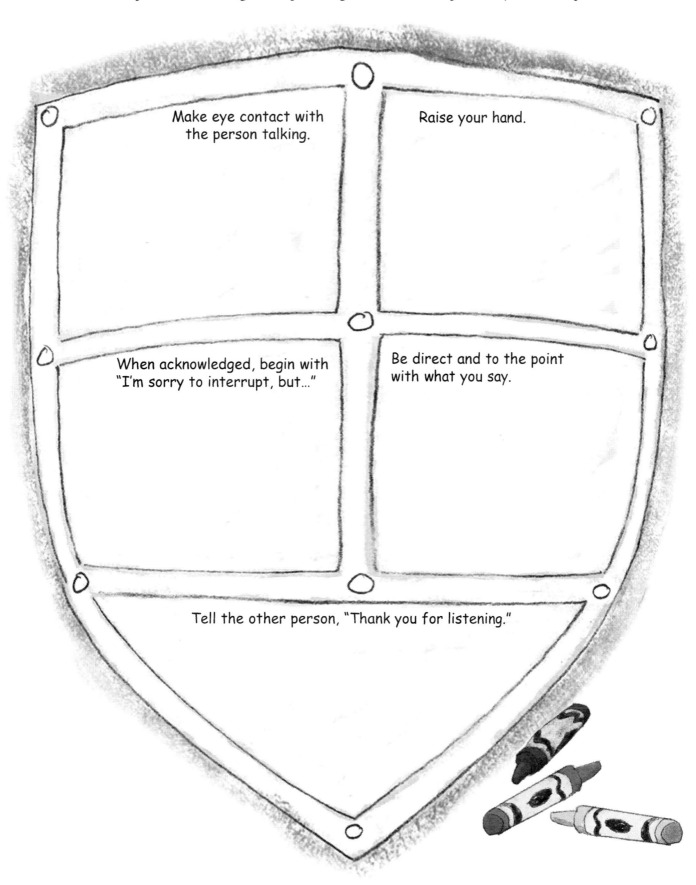

Make eye contact with the person talking.

Raise your hand.

When acknowledged, begin with "I'm sorry to interrupt, but..."

Be direct and to the point with what you say.

Tell the other person, "Thank you for listening."

"SQUOOOZE" IT OR LOSE IT

Many times students think of things to say while direct teaching is taking place. They quickly raise their hands and wait to be called on. If the teacher is in the middle of a teaching concept he/she may not want to call on students. The students then begin to fixate on what they want to say. They want to be heard, and they certainly don't want to forget their very important words. Students become so focused on their contributions that they fail to listen to the direct teaching.

Teach your students to "SQUOOOZE IT OR LOSE IT!!"

Narrative:
The next time I am in the middle of teaching a lesson, and you think of something important to say, look at me and raise your hand, If I don't call on you right away, "SQUOOOZE" what you want to say by placing your idea between your fingers and crossing them. Put your crossed fingers in your lap. Lower your hand, and wait. When I finish talking, raise your hand. When I call on you, uncross your fingers and let your "SQUOOOZED" thoughts out.

If you learn to be a good "SQUOOOZER" you will never forget what you want to say, and you will be able to listen more effectively when I am teaching.

Practice and model "SQUOOOZING" with your students several times.

SQUOOOZE

VOLCANO COMICS—YOU BE THE ARTIST!

Directions: In each box, draw your own cartoon using the prompt given.

Draw Louis erupting.

Words pop into my head, and slide down onto my tongue.	My tummy starts to rumble and grumble! My words begin to wiggle and giggle!	My tongue pushes all my words into my teeth…and I ERUPT!

Draw Louis learning to control his eruption.

I bite down hard!	I blow my words out through my nose and wait for my turn.	I breathe my words back into my mouth and say what I need to say.

YOU FILL IT IN

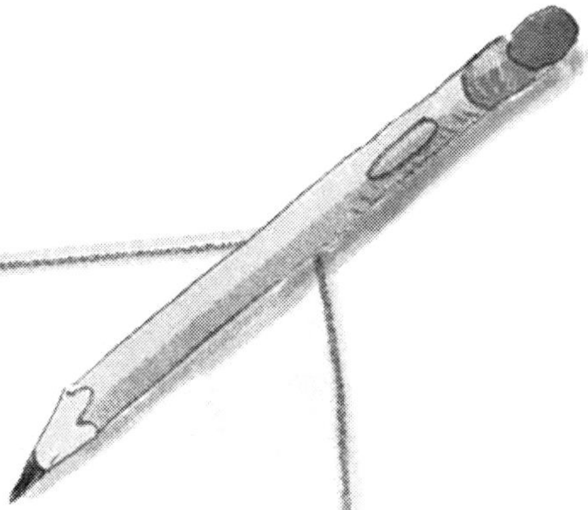

When I interrupt someone, it makes me feel _____

because _____ .

_____

When other people interrupt me, it makes me feel_____

because _____ .

_____

When I interrupt at home, my parents _____ .

_____

When I interrupt at school, my teacher _____ .

_____

When other kids interrupt in my class, my teacher _____ .

because_____

Kids who interrupt all the time have a hard time _____ .

_____

I interrupt sometimes because_____ .

_____

Sometimes you need to interrupt, like when _____ .

_____

I can get myself out of the habit of interrupting others by _____ .

_____

The best way to teach people not to interrupt others is to _____ .

_____

BUILD a Volcano!

Materials Needed

- One empty toilet paper roll
- Two small plastic baggies
- One Tissue
- Tape
- 4 cups flour

- 1 cup salt
- 1-1/2 cups warm tap water
- 1 tsp vegetable oil
- Food coloring
- Baking soda

- Poster board or piece of cardboard
- Powdered sugar
- Vinegar
- One rubber band

Directions

To Make the Volcano

1. Tape the toilet paper roll to the poster board as shown (Fig. A).
2. Line one of the plastic baggies with the tissue.
3. Place the other plastic baggie inside the first baggie so that the tissue acts as a divider between them.
4. Make a liner for the toilet paper roll by placing the plastic baggie into the top of the roll with the edges folded over the top of the roll. Secure baggies with rubber band as shown (Fig. B).
5. Add food coloring to the water until the mixture is a dark brown.
6. Mix flour, salt, oil, and colored water to form dough. (Add more food coloring if needed.)
7. Mold dough around the tube to form the volcano as shown.
8. Let the volcano dry (approx. 5 days).

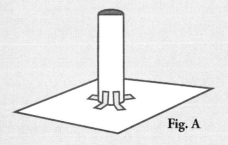

Fig. A

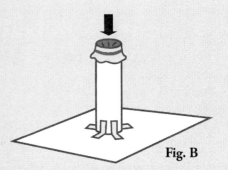

Fig. B

To Prepare the Eruption:

1. Fill the top baggie with baking soda (approx. 2 heaping tablespoons).
2. Mix 1 cup vinegar with red and yellow food coloring to achieve the desired color of lava. Set aside ½ cup of mixture for Step 6.
3. Carefully pour colored vinegar into the baggie (mouth) of your volcano and watch it ERUPT! This symbolizes Louis before he learned to control his important words.
4. When your eruption is over, carefully lift the first baggie out of the tube and throw it away. Discard the tissue as well.
5. Fill the second baggie with two heaping tablespoons of powdered sugar.
6. Pour the reserved liquid from Step 2 into the mouth of your volcano. Point out to the students that an eruption doesn't take place. This symbolizes Louis after he learned to control his very important words.

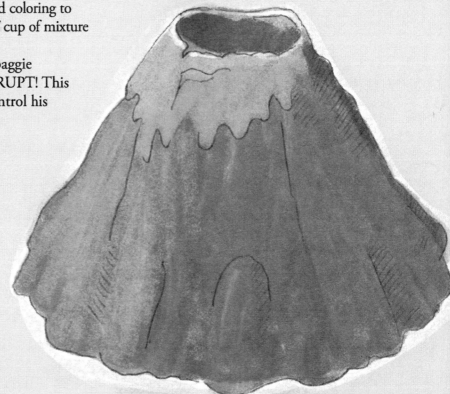

WRITING EXTENSIONS

Instructions

Choose one of the ideas below and write a short story.

Teacher: When students are finished, have them present their stories to the class, without interrupting of course!

- **How do you think Bill's bubble gum got stuck in Louis' hair? Write a story explaining how this happened.**

- **Sometimes we find ourselves in situations where interrupting is necessary. Write about a time when this has happened to you. What might have happened if you had not interrupted? (Teachers: brainstorm with students situations that may arise when they may need to interrupt; i.e. someone is in danger or time is a factor etc.)**

- **I Can't Believe This Is Happening To Me! Pretend that you have a volcano mouth. Write a story about your words and how they keep exploding out of your mouth. Do you get into trouble for interrupting? How do you get rid of your volcano mouth? At the end of your story, draw a picture of yourself with a volcano mouth.**

- **Louis was very upset when his classmates interrupted him on his very important day. Has that ever happened to you? Write about a time when someone interrupted you. How did it make you feel?**

- **Louis' sister Sylvia tells LONG winded "girl" stories at the dinner table. Become Sylvia and tell us what she is saying.**

- **Write a story explaining what might happen if everyone interrupted all of the time.**

BREAK THE CODE

Using the key on the left, decode the following secret messages. Write each letter above the symbol. (See the bottom of the page for answers.)

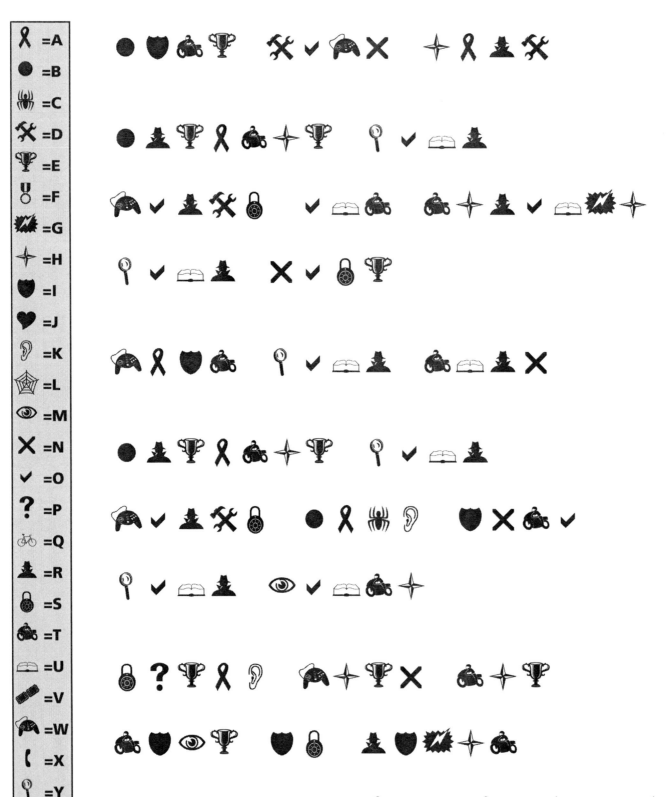

PROMOTION TIME!

You are an advertising executive. Your boss just handed you the following assignment:
Using the billboard space below, design a billboard to advertise and promote the book:

My Mouth is a Volcano!

BE CREATIVE!
(Rumble, Grumble, Wiggle,
Jiggle, Bite Down Really Hard, Etc.)

LUCKY BUTTON

There are times when it really helps to have a reminder! A lucky button is any button that you choose threaded onto a string like a necklace. When you need a special reminder not to interrupt, wear your lucky button around your neck. Lucky buttons really work, but only if you believe in their power!

Material Needed:
- Miscellaneous buttons
- String

MAKE IT FIT

Materials Needed:
- Glue
- Poster Board (1 per small group)
- Brown lunch sacks each packed with the following items:
  - Band aid
  - Rubber band
  - Toothpick
  - Paper clip
  - Hard mint candy (wrapped)
  - Stick of gum (wrapped)
  - Penny
  - Life saver (wrapped)

Directions:
Divide into small groups of about four students. Give each group a poster board and a sack full of items as noted above. Have groups work together to create a poster using the items in the bag that reflect what they have learned from *My Mouth is a Volcano!* The poster can serve as an advertisement for the book. You must use all items. Be creative!

Examples:
- The stick of gum can symbolize your lips sticking together
- The penny could symbolize "common sense (cents)"
- The life saver could symbolize what Louis' mom is to him for teaching him how not to interrupt

THE CONSEQUENCES ARE...

Pretend that Louis has not learned how to control his interrupting.
Below list four consequences that can happen to him when he continues to interrupt.
Draw a picture of your favorite consequence.

1. _____

2. _____

3. _____

4. _____

MORE THAN WORDS

Our author wants you to be her new illustrator.
In each box, draw a picture that goes with the words
from the story *My Mouth is a Volcano*.

[drawing box]

I Erupt! Words just explode out of my mouth. My mouth is a volcano!!!

[drawing box]

As soon as my sister finished talking, I took a deep breath, and back in went the words.
I was amazed that they had just hung around outside my mouth and didn't float away.
Then I told my story, and nobody got mad at me for erupting.

WHAT CAN YOU MAKE OF IT?

How many words (two or more letters) can you make of the letters found in *My Mouth is a Volcano!*
Write your answers below.

My Mouth is a Volcano!

1. _____

2. _____

3. _____

4. _____

5. _____

6. _____

7. _____

8. _____

9. _____

10. _____

11. _____

12. _____

13. _____

14. _____

15. _____

16. _____

17. _____

18. _____

19. _____

20. _____

21. _____

22. _____

23. _____

24. _____

YOU BE THE AUTHOR

Our author is out sick, and we need your help! Below each picture, write two sentences for the illustration. Think about how Louis feels in each and the lesson(s) he has learned about controlling his erupting voice.

_____

_____

_____

_____

_____

_____